THE CUCK

ARON BEAUREGARD

ISBN: 9798421173106

Cover & Interior Art by Anton Rosovsky

Cover wrap design by Don Noble

Edited by Patrick C. Harrison III, Mort Stone,
& Candace Nola

Printed in the USA

Maggot Press
Coventry, Rhode Island

WARNING:
This book contains scenes and subject matter
that are disgusting and disturbing, easily
offended people are not the intended audience

JOIN MY MAGGOT MAILING LIST NOW
FOR EXCLUSIVE OFFERS AND UPDATES
BY EMAILING:
AronBeauregardHorror@gmail.com

FOR SIGNED BOOKS, MERCHANDISE,
AND EXCLUSIVE ITEMS VISIT:

www.ABHorror.com

For Meatball Mike

"I like to prowl ordinary places and taste the people—from a distance."

- Charles Bukowski

ON A WASTED WHIM

Ben and Mickey looked down at their pints with excitement leeched onto their pupils. The beautiful near-black stout remained hypnotic, despite their sloppy mannerisms showcasing they'd clearly had their fill already. In unison, the pair held shot glasses full of Irish cream above their beers, inebriated grins gracing their faces.

"To Mickey and Ava! Cheers!" Ben shouted.

From the corner of his eye, Mickey could see the bartender's patience wearing thin.

"Relax, it was just a conversation. I don't even have a date yet; we're far from wedding bells," Mickey replied.

"You're due, you're fuckin' due, mate."

"Don't get my hopes up," Mickey said, relinquishing his tender grip on the shot glass.

Ben followed suit, releasing his, probably from higher up than was sensical. The thick Guinness erupted around the edge of the glass, splattering all over the counter and onto Ben's lap. They each speedily snatched up their foaming beverages and chugged.

In just seconds, the entire body of alcohol in each of the generous glasses had vanished and their chins were wet with pleasure.

"Alright, I've had about enough of the bullshit! It's time the two of you boys hit the bricks," the bartender barked.

"We—We just want one more," Ben pleaded, slurring his words.

"You got a fuckin' hearing problem? Square up and fuck off, or I'll give you one more, but it won't be the one you're thinking."

The bartender cracked his deformed knuckles; a red flag that indicated it would be wise to heed his warning.

"Alright, mate, alright," Mickey said, pulling a few pounds from his wallet and laying them in the froth on the counter.

"I ain't your fucking mate."

"Well, with that kind of service, don't expect a tip."

"Chill, Ben," Mickey ordered, not looking to deal with an altercation that evening.

"Are you still fucking here?! Piss off!" the bartender rebutted, extracting a small wooden bat from underneath the bar.

The sight of the weapon in the bartender's hand and the malice in his eyes was enough to motivate them. They stumbled out of the pub and onto the chilly, slick sidewalk.

"Fuck me, that bloke thinks he's hot shit. He should be getting these hands right now," Ben muttered.

"Whenever you put a few drinks away you seem to forget, you're the lover and I'm the fighter. But you bloody well talk like you're Mike Tyson. It wouldn't be your knuckles that are all torn up tomorrow, it'd be mine. I'm trying to be the lover for once. So, if you plan on starting that shit, you better be ready to fight," Mickey joked, elevating his hands and falling into his boxing stance.

Sure, it was a joke, but in reality, there was more truth to it than there had been in the past. Mickey wasn't looking to scrap over pints, he was looking to connect with Ava.

"What, you think 'cause I'm good with the ladies that I won't put you down?" Ben laughed, throwing a jab into Mickey's chest.

FREE

Mickey slapped the light punch away with ease.

"Don't test me, you won't like the outcome."

Ben backed up toward the telephone pole and a rectangular metal box, containing some free flyers inside. He threw a second playful jab at Mickey. It landed on his shoulder, in turn generating a grin and allowing his crooked teeth to project.

"Now you've done it," Mickey said, jolting forward in a flash and tackling Ben into the flyer receptacle.

The container tipped over and a half-dozen of the free pamphlets spilled onto the moist sidewalk. As Mickey spiritedly mounted Ben, and continued to belt him with ginger blows, Ben's eyes happened upon the cracked open back-pages of the periodicals.

"Wait, wait!" Ben cried.

"Had enough already?" Mickey asked.

"Let's get fucked. What do you say?"

"What nonsense are you speaking about now?"

The two lethargically disengaged and Ben pointed to a three-inch inky square on the back of the magazine. It read: 'CALL FOR FREE FUN. LOOKING FOR A MAN WHO DOESN'T MIND LARGER LADIES.'

"A sex ad? Are you out of your skull?" Mickey asked, pulling himself to his feet.

"Why not?! It's all in good fun, mate," Ben replied, lifting himself up along with the paper.

"No, Ben. I've never done it before and don't plan on starting tonight."

"Just because you've never done it before doesn't mean you can't start now! It's fuckin' nineteen-ninety-seven, mate! The decade's almost over! Grow a pair before it's too late!"

"I ain't phoning no back-page sex ad."

Ben smirked; he knew that he had him right where he wanted him now. He would've bet his life on it. Mickey's tune had changed ever so slightly. His friend was no longer outright denying partaking in the perversion, but merely saying he wouldn't initiate the assembly.

"You don't have to, I'll call. Please, I haven't had a lay in days!" Ben whined.

"Days? Try months you twat—"

"All the more reason for you to come with me! You need a lay. You need to prime yourself before you meet up with Ava. Don't wanna be popping your load on the first pump; that would kill things before they begin."

Mickey remained silent. He knew Ben was a pervert; a sex-fueled nymphomaniac. Coming across ladies was a hard thing for someone as rough and rugged as Mickey. He had a face that garnered pity, not pussy. As illogical as Ben could be in most moments, he was actually making sense.

"C'mon, when's the last time you had a true adventure?! A bold 'fuck-it-all' moment that you woke up laughing about? This is gonna help you. This is what life's all about, mate."

Mickey looked down at Ben's hands. He stared at the phone number under the font.

"You'll call?"

"Anything for you, friend," Ben replied, smiling like sunshine lasering through a window.

He was clever with his words and had a knack for always getting what he wanted. Ben's manipulation tactics were never anything malicious, but his whimsical ideas had landed them in hot water before. But it was that exact breed of delinquency that had also drawn Mickey to Ben. It was why they'd become such great friends in the first place.

The crooked grin that had vacated Mickey's face suddenly flared up again.

"Fuck it, let's find a payphone."

THE CUCK

They pulled up to the curb of the dark street just after one in the morning. Ben parked the car a reasonable distance from the outwardly spacious but weathered house. The road itself had many trees and the handful of properties on that particular block were spread out generously.

"This is fucking perfect, mate," Ben whispered, looking behind them and taking comfort in the quiet emptiness of their general circumference.

"Perfect? House looks like it belongs to fucking Ian Brady," Mickey whined.

"Ah, stop your belly-aching."

"So, you'll go in first?"

"No, we both go in. She said she wants us both."

"I don't know… What if she's got something?"

"That's why you've got your fucking rubber then, innit? Don't puss out on me now. Besides, you're already out of the car and I hold the keys. You don't have a choice anymore."

Mickey stopped his protest and quietly followed the path down the side of the house as he'd been instructed to.

"What's her name?" Mickey whispered.

"That's a good question. You'll have to ask her," Ben

replied, moving a semi-cracked flowerpot to the side near the bulkhead door.

"Here it is," Ben whispered, lifting a small rusty key off the ground.

"This is fucking stupid—"

"Shut your bloody mouth. Keep quiet," Ben interrupted, fitting the key into the hole.

The door squeaked open and a gateway to darkness appeared before them. The rain that had stopped for close to an hour abruptly picked back up again.

"This is it. Follow me."

Ben descended the cement steps until he reached the bottom. The blackness that besieged him was a degree that his pupils had yet to properly adjust to.

"Close it behind you."

"Are you mad?" Mickey asked.

"The fucking rain! She told me to close it anyhow. You don't have to lock it, just set it shut."

Mickey pulled the door closed behind them and joined Ben at the bottom of the dirty stairs. He struggled to make out his next steps amid the darkness.

"Now what?"

"She—She said her bedroom's the first door on the left once we go up the stairs. Wherever the fuck those are."

Suddenly, a light flickered, and a flame appeared just a few paces away from them. The orangey glow illuminated a face that was both leathery and unsettling.

The man was older, probably in his sixties. His oversized Coke-bottle glasses reflected the flame dancing up from the lighter below. His eyes were dark and his erratic, pointy teeth sprung in many directions within the opening of his mouth. His skin was quite gristly and wrinkled with decades of stress and turmoil. The lighter in his hand shook ever so slightly, but his long, spiked thumbnail held fast on the fork, keeping the flame alive.

"Ahhhhhh!"

"Fuck!"

Both Ben and Mickey were instantly stricken with fear. Instinctually, Ben jumped, and Mickey turned right back for the bulkhead door.

"Wait, lads! It's okay! You've come to the right place. Sorry if I startled you, 'twas not my intent. As you might imagine, we get the occasional weirdos that come by. I like to just get a quick look before bringing them up to my Bessie. Apologies for the lighter, the electrical in the basement shorted. Better that than the bog, I suppose," the old man said with a chuckle.

"She—She's your wife?" Mickey asked, now just as confused as he was concerned.

"Afraid so. She's a lovely gal. Don't worry, she's much younger than me. She is a pinch on the heavy side, but she's warm as any."

"Forgive the boldness of this question, but why would you want us to fuck your wife?" Mickey asked, slurring his question a tad.

"Well, things aren't exactly working proper down there for me anymore. Furthermore, my relationship with Bessie has never really been a physical one. We're more life partners than anything. It's kind of an odd thing, which is why we're not really up front about it. But if it's all the same, I just want to see her happy. I want to see my lady pleased. I like to watch her be pleased."

"He's a fuckin' cuck," Ben mumbled, finding himself a bit annoyed by the old bastard.

Mickey elbowed him. It seemed his drunken antics never failed, regardless of how bizarre the nature of the situation they walked into.

"That's not what we agreed to with Bessie," Ben said, unhappy with the new terms.

"I understand that, but think about it, lad. You fellas can do what you like, she loves the attention. I'll just be in the corner. You won't hear a peep out of me. I promise."

Mickey and Ben both looked at each other, a bit baffled by the proposition.

"Please, help an old man out, fellas. I beg you."

The eerie flame continued to glow beneath his wrinkly chin. The Cuck slurped up a bit of saliva from the corner of his mouth. His old tongue ran a few revolutions over his lips as he watched them debate the idea.

Ben looked into Mickey's eyes.

"I frankly don't give a fuck about the geezer. I say we just have a few minutes of fun. We're already here."

Mickey seemed more apprehensive. The old weirdo bothered him. He didn't know the reason, only that it wasn't the same reason that bothered Ben. He could tell he was annoyed, but not worried in the slightest. Mickey was always a little worried. Because he knew that if things went to shit, he'd be the one cleaning it up.

Mickey stared at the old man's warped remaining teeth, visible via the flicker.

"Fuck it," Mickey mumbled.

"Exactly! Now follow me this way. Just one other thing, my Bessie doesn't like it to be loud. So, just try and keep it down. Have as much fun as you like but do it quietly. I'll do the same. You won't hear a peep out of me once we go into her bedroom. It'll be like I'm not even there."

When they arrived in front of the door, the old man pointed toward it, gesturing them to open it and enter.

Ben took the lead, grabbing his crotch with anticipation. When he opened the door, the old man followed him in, and as promised, filed into the far corner of the gloomy room. Mickey looked behind them at the dim kitchen, and stairwell beyond it, before quietly closing the door.

What lay on the bed was a far cry from what they'd hoped. Bessie was a behemoth. She laid completely nude on the king-size mattress, her body so large that she probably couldn't have rolled out of bed without assistance. The layers of doughy fat weighed Bessie down, leaving her warped casing distending in various directions. Her goliath gut oozed around both her enormous thighs and drooped downward, covering her substantial slit.

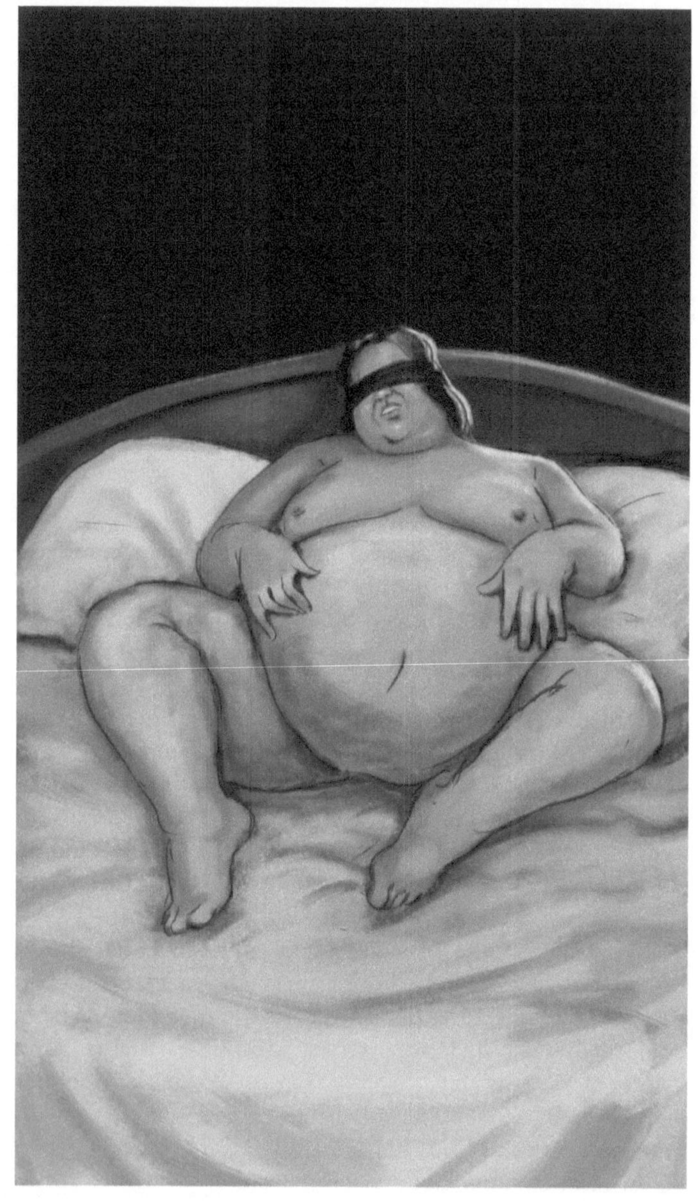

Her long black hair was sprawled outward all around the pillow her hearty head was laid upon. Interestingly, she'd decided to blindfold herself. A piece of burgundy cloth was tightly wrapped around her head just above her sharp nose.

Upon hearing the door and footsteps, Bessie quickly rolled her head to the side.

"Ben, is that you?" she asked, her mouth manipulated by a toothy grin of excitement.

As they approached the front of the bed, Ben's expression was no longer one of drop-dead anticipation. However, he was still fiending to release his demons and was ready, nonetheless.

"It is, darling," he said, looking over to Mickey with wide-eyes that screamed 'this is one for the record books.'

"So glad that you found me. Did you bring Mickey here too?"

"Of course, dear, he wouldn't miss this for the world."

"Hi, Mickey," Bessie whispered.

"H—Hi," Mickey replied awkwardly.

Mickey was glad they'd drank so damn much, otherwise he might not be able to go through with it. But the fact was that he'd been without pussy for some time. The situation wasn't ideal, but he was too fucking wasted to care. He kept hearing Ben's conniving voice in his cranium: 'You need to prime yourself before you meet up with Ava.'

"Thank you again, fellas, for coming to see me. You can do most anything. I'm not a picky gal. The only thing I ask is that you keep this hush. Don't be too loud, okay?"

"I think we can manage that," Ben said, dropping his trousers.

"Well, come on then," Bessie said, grabbing a piece of pillow beside her and sticking it inside her mouth.

After finding enough drunken balance to roll on his rubber, Ben wasted little time in inserting himself into Bessie's slimy hole. The heat of her hearty walls was true. The Cuck was right; she was warm as any.

Due to Bessie's incredible size, there wasn't much wiggle

room for creativity with fancy positions. Ben didn't see an issue; he just went all in the old-fashioned way. He closed his eyes and gritted his teeth, pounding away at her meaty muff like a stray dog that had found a fix. Ben used the images of his past flings to fight his way through the lay and enjoy every minute of it. His intoxication and imagination assisted him in building up to a surging climax.

As he released his load into his lambskin, Bessie struggled not to squeal out. Her jaws clamped firm on the edge of the pillow while she subdued her audible satisfaction.

While Ben pulled out and got his condom off, Mickey couldn't help but glance over at the old man in the corner.

His tongue was even wetter than before. The oddly thin muscle flailed around his lips and leapt out past his razor-teeth. The dribble escaped him further and coincided with the dry-rubbing of his spikey fingernails upon his crotch.

Bessie exhaled deeply and pulled the saliva-saturated pillow out of her mouth.

"Heavens, I was almost there," she whispered.

"Well, maybe next time. Or maybe old Mickey here can pull you up that mountain," Ben said, slapping his friend on the back with a smile.

"I would *love* that," Bessie begged.

Mickey snapped out of the trance-like state the old weirdo had sent him spiraling into. The alcohol fueled him so effectively, it allowed him to switch gears and concentrate on the task at hand.

Mickey wrestled his pants and boxers down and sloppily slid on his protection. As was the case for Ben, Mickey had only one option for entry. He stared at the runny opening as the sudsy, feminine fluids dripped out in creamy dollops. The hole had already been warmed up for him when Mickey began to pump furiously.

In and out.

In and out.

In and out.

Unlike Ben, Mickey found himself attracted to Bessie. Bigger girls were quite beautiful to him, so as his excitement surged, so did Bessie's. There was an unspoken connection, an organic sexuality that manifested upon the joining of their genitalia. Mickey sent a flurry of relentless thrusts, seeming like he might never reach exhaustion.

Mickey watched Bessie quiver with bliss, and he knew that he had brought her up the mountain. It was splendid timing, because he could restrain his ejaculation no longer. As the gunky sperm flooded out of his urethra, Mickey unintentionally turned his head.

Regrettably, his gaze locked with The Cuck in the corner. He was every bit as disgusted by the bastard as he was just moments before. But something was different. Mickey found himself even more disturbed than he'd been prior to his plunge inside Bessie. Even his muddled mind could tell that The Cuck's eyes didn't look the same.

They were darker.

They were deader.

They were black.

How bloody drunk am I? Mickey wondered as an injection of ultra-uncomfortable dread molested him.

"Oh, Mickey," Bessie cried.

The muffled squeal turned his attention back to her.

"That was incredible. Fucking to the moon incredible," she said, letting her exhaustion be known. "But I—I want more…"

"Sorry, dear, it's past two in the mornin' now. It's been lovely, but we've got to get on," Ben said, taking a few strides towards the door.

Mickey dismounted Bessie and chaotically composed himself while Ben sneered at the creepy old man still hovering in the corner and opened the door.

The Cuck was still now, appearing almost frozen in time. He stared back at the boys with a gleeful grin, as his human gravy continued to expel from his upsetting orifice. His presence remained bothersome.

"Maybe you can call me again sometime then?" Bessie sheepishly suggested.

"We've got your number. Mickey, come on now."

"Alright, it was a pleasure. Please be sure to leave quietly and lock the door for me on the way out."

"Of course."

Ben saw that Mickey was still having a hell of a time getting his bearings. Thankfully, he'd finally gotten his trousers buckled up. Ben reached out and grabbed Mickey by the arm, carefully leading him out of the room the same way they'd come in.

"I'm ready to get the fuck home now," Ben whispered.

The pair stumbled through the basement door and down the wooden steps as quietly as their inebriation allowed. When they entered the darkness of the cellar again, it was a bit easier to find their path to the bulkhead door. Ben pushed it open, and the rain connected with his face, but before he exited, he heard the The Cuck's voice again.

"It's been a bloody pleasure, boys. Hopefully, I'll see you around," he said, sucking up the drool from his lips.

He was close enough that they could smell an aroma that Ben and Mickey couldn't quite put their fingers on. It was almost smoky, like he'd just returned from a weekend of campfire tales.

They both turned back and looked at his unnerving expression. The lighter had reignited, and the glow of his features evoked an odd feeling of discomfort in each of their guts. Looking upon The Cuck was like having an irritated sandworm squirming under your skin.

Neither Ben nor Mickey said another word to him. They simply continued on, closing the bulkhead behind them. His words had fallen flat, as they didn't plan on seeing the spooky old man ever again.

THE UNWANTED

When the phone rang, it reverberated violently in Mickey's mind, feeling like a bell hanging inside his cranium was being savagely struck. He shuffled about in his bed, struggling to allow his blurry and crusted vision to come into focus. The profound dread at the thought of another debilitating work day echoed about in his fragile psyche. Mickey lethargically reached for the phone and finally lifted it off the receiver.

"My bloody skull feels like it might come apart," Ben said in a voice that one might use to call out of the office.

"Yeah, you're telling me. At least you don't have to work today," Mickey mumbled.

"Can't believe we fucking did that, mate. You're crazy."

"Me? It was your god-awful idea. I just wanted a few drinks, some conversation. Next thing I know I'm knee-deep in one of your shameful plots."

"It all worked out, innit?"

"I suppose."

"Now when Ava gives you a ring, you'll be ready to tango."

"We'll see. It's been about a week already and still nothing. I don't even know why I was excited last night."

"If she doesn't ring then just call her already. You're the man; you're supposed to make the move. You've waited long enough."

"I'm not in any kind of shape to be talking to her, thanks to you."

"Jesus, I go out of my way to prepare you for love, and this is the thanks I get? I've done you a favour by my count. Show me a little appreciation, why don't you?"

"I've gotta take a shower."

"Same. I'm fixing to pick up where I left off last night."

"You can't be serious. You're going back to Bessie's flat?"

"Fuck no, not with her. Olivia's popping in for a liquid lunch."

"Well, better straighten up then. You want her to have a drink with you, not be playing catch-up."

"I'll be ready. She's just got some new piercings on her nipples. Can't wait to have a look."

"Right, well, I've got to be off and shovel shit for the day. Enjoy your day off, fucking wanker."

Mickey hung up the phone and looked at his work boots. He let out a depressed sigh and lifted himself out of bed.

***

The factory was cold and unforgiving. Mickey was bundled up as best he could, but the tips of his toes remained cold. He used the nail gun to construct the wooden pallets, heaping them up in a pile beside his station. Every few minutes or so the forklift coasted inside to lift up his constructions, then disappeared.

The process was so redundant that he could've done the fucking job on acid. Maybe that was one of the things he enjoyed about it though. His mind was free to wander.

The last few days he'd spent thinking almost non-stop about Ava. The sweet girl at the coffee shop that he'd gone out of his way to keep bumping into made his heart flutter.

Mickey had been on cloud nine for days. Despite nothing having happened yet, just the mere prospect that it could was enough to eradicate the moldy depression that had been festering upon his cerebellum since he could recall. After finally mustering the willpower to suggest exchanging phone numbers, Mickey found himself constantly battling with waiting for her to call, verses initiating it. He didn't want to seem desperate, but it had been almost a week and he was growing a smidge concerned.

But that morning was different than the prior six.

Ava, and the thoughts of what they might do if they decided to get together, hadn't even flashed in his head. All he could think about was the debauchery of the prior evening. More specifically, the disturbing way The Cuck had visually ingested him.

For that moment, the twisted bastard's peepers looked ebony. He couldn't seem to shake the image out of his head.

Eyes of oblivion.

A picture of dread.

Mickey couldn't shake the feeling that he'd stared directly into something he couldn't explain. Harsh uncertainty bombarded him. He wasn't a fella that spent a lot of time dwelling on the past or wondering. Why did he feel so disturbed? It was as if the gateway to damnation had swung open before him.

How could they be black? The room was dark, but they looked blacker than the room. It's illogical...

No matter how many times he attempted to shift his mindset, as sure as he plunged nails into the planks in front of him, The Cuck remained in his thoughts.

***

When Mickey returned back to his flat, he heard a faint noise sneaking its way through the wooden door leading into his apartment. He struggled to make it out but didn't compute what it was until he opened the door.

The phone was ringing!

"Ava!"

His heart raced as the ring died out. He lifted the phone off the receiver, only to be bombarded with a dial tone of disappointment. They'd given up.

"Shit! Of course! Just my luck!"

Mickey set the phone back down on the receiver and exhaled his sadness. He moseyed over to the door and closed it a little more aggressively than he normally would have.

He glanced into the mirror that sat atop his dresser, the melancholic feeling manipulating his expression.

"I guess it's up to you then, fella."

Suddenly, the phone rang again. Mickey rushed over to his bedside and answered it before the second ring could complete.

"Hello?" he said, voice sounding a tad more on the tender side than was typical.

"I think something's wrong, horribly wrong, Mickey."

"Ben? Wait, did you just call me a few seconds ago?"

"No, but I need to—"

"I think Ava's trying to call me now, I'm gonna have to get back to you in a few—"

"Mate, fuckin' listen to me! Trust me, she can wait! This is far more important…"

Ben's tone was different than it normally was. Mickey was picking up on an emotional accent that he'd never really heard him express so straightforwardly; it was fear.

"Alright, settle down. What's the issue?"

"I can't stop thinking about last night, it's—it's like it's happening all over again."

"You mean Bessie?"

"No, the fuckin' cuck."

"What the hell are you talking about?"

"Olivia came over today as planned. Everything was going wonderful. Had a few drinks, a bit of a talk, it was all perfect until…"

"Until what?"

"Until we started to fuck. When I first went inside her, I felt it. It was faint at first, you know, like when you think you're alone but can't shake the feeling that someone's watching you? I shrugged it off and continued some, but the feeling… it just wouldn't go away. The more I tried not to think about it, the more I couldn't help myself."

"Think about what?"

"That slimy old bastard watching me. Even though I was fuckin' Olivia, I could still see him in my mind. Then I could smell him. That same out-of-place smoky smell that was there when we left the basement last night. I could hear him suckling his drool back up from his cracked lips. It was like he was fuckin' there mate. And then he was."

Mickey laughed, but quickly got a little angry. He knew Ava might have been trying to reach him at that very moment, and Ben was taking the piss.

"I told you that Ava might be trying to call me, and you go on with all that, pulling my chain. What kind of asshole are you?"

"It ain't a fuckin' joke, mate! That's what I'm trying to tell you! He was there! He was fuckin' there, standing in the corner! Watching me!"

Mickey's face transitioned to display his concern. The things Ben was saying were unlike him. He joked around from time to time, but never in such a methodical and practical manner. In all the time they'd known each other, this was a first. He knew there was something wrong, but the source of the problem was still up for debate.

"Ben, are you having some kind of a nervous breakdown or something? You know I love you, bro, but this is just shit timing."

"Why would I lie to you?"

"Okay, so if he was there, what did Olivia say?"

"She… she couldn't see him."

"She couldn't see him?"

"Only I could."

"Jesus Christ, you know how this sounds, right? I mean put yourself in my shoes."

"Fine. Don't believe me. I'm not sure that it even matters anyway."

"Maybe you're just tired? Maybe we need to slow down. We both might've been on one too many benders. Sleep depravity can cause people to hallucinate, amongst other weird shit."

"He was there. Sure as I'm talking to you right now, he was fuckin' there."

"You said he *was* there; where did he go? Did he just walk out your front door, all willy-nilly?"

"No."

"Then what happened?"

"It's gonna sound crazy…"

"We're already at fuckin' crazy, mate."

"It's gonna sound crazier. Crazier than you're thinking."

"Try me."

"He disappeared."

"He—He did what now?"

"After I stopped having sex with Olivia, he vanished. He disappeared."

Ben spoke with such a matter-of-fact candor that it chilled Mickey to the core. He couldn't help but feel like his friend was in a real bad spot.

"You know what, you're right. Ava can wait. I'm—I'm gonna head over. You're seriously starting to fuckin' worry me now, mate."

There was a pause on the line as Ben reassessed the situation. He understood that he was causing a lot of trouble on his friend's side.

"No, maybe you're right. Maybe my head is just all fucked up. It sounds so crazy. Yeah… you're right. I want you to call Ava. I can't take that away from you. I'm just— I'm gonna get some rest, maybe that'll help."

"You're sure? You being okay is more important than a phone call. A phone call can wait."

"No, this was… it was good. I think I just needed to talk to someone."

"Alright, but if you need anything, just ring me back, deal?"

"Deal."

"Okay, later then."

"Bye."

Mickey didn't want to let him go. In a way, he felt like he was failing Ben, but he wasn't sure what else he could do. He seemed to be grasping reality again. Mickey couldn't help but recall how much The Cuck had been on his mind that day as well.

Internally, he couldn't agree more with Ben. The old weirdo was creepy as hell. His face hovering in that darkness paired with his naturally nasty features left a seed of strangeness swelling inside him that continued to grow. But there was a big difference in thinking about The Cuck for a few hours during his work shift, and actually saying he was standing right there beside him.

Just as the receiver touched down on the phone, it began to ring again. With fear still flowing through his frame, Mickey snatched the phone back up.

"Hello?"

"Hello, is Mickey there?" the soft, feminine voice asked.

"Yes, he is, I—I mean this is him."

Mickey smacked his palm against his forehead; he was already stumbling out of the gate.

Play it cool, just relax.

"Hey there! It's Ava, from The Bean Shop."

"Oh, Ava! Great to hear from you."

"Same. Anyhow, as I was wrapping up my shift today, it dawned on me that I'm a bit thirsty. I wonder if you might be interested in grabbing a drink tonight?"

Mickey's eyes widened. He was thrilled, but also pretty exhausted. Back-to-back benders weren't a wise thing, but the moment he heard her voice, he knew he'd be doing whatever she asked.

"Just name the place," he said with a grin.

23

HOT DATE

Of all the places she had to pick the pub that Mickey and Ben had been tossed out of just an evening prior. The bartender took his time getting to them and continued to give Mickey the evil eye. The bad vibes were breaking his concentration; he wanted to seem as interesting as possible. After a good five minutes of chit-chat, finally, the bartender approached them.

"You, again. You gonna behave tonight?" the bartender asked, with a hint of discontent.

Ava's eyes popped a tad, but she found the comment comical.

"Not sure what you're referring to," Mickey said, trying to play it off as best he could.

"You're lucky you've brought a pretty face with you," the grizzled poison pourer said, winking at Ava. "So, what'll it be then?"

"Couple pints of Guinness, please," Mickey replied.

The bartender turned around and stepped toward the draft spouts without saying another word.

"Wow, they're friendly in here," Mickey joked.

"I see someone's got a good reputation around these parts," Ava said with a smile.

"It's not what you think."

"Oh yeah? Then what is it?"

"I was in here last night with me mate, Ben. He can be a little much once he's had a few. Hopefully you'll get to meet him at some point."

Finally, Ben was good for something besides trouble. With him absent, at the very least Mickey could drop the blame on his lap.

"That's okay, I can be a bit much too, at times. A little trouble is healthy, it can make you feel alive."

Ava looked back over toward the bartender as he let the head from each pour settle.

"Should we get shots too?"

***

Mickey and Ava burst through the door of his apartment mid-embrace, both clearly sloshed, the spirits powering their primal instincts. In the darkness, she tongued him wildly, like kissing him was essential to stabilize her heartbeat. The door slammed shut and their clothes came off. Mickey laid her on the bed and dragged his kisses down to her toned abdomen.

Just as his nose dropped past her belly button, the flickers invaded his mind:

The Cuck's rotten teeth.

The Cuck's pointed yellow fingernails.

The Cuck's drool-drenched thrashing tongue.

The Cuck's blackened sockets of abyss.

"What the fuck?" Mickey whispered.

"Yeah, I wanna fuck. I thought it was obvious," Ava eagerly replied while sliding out of her panties.

Mickey tried to shake off the cobwebs that had suddenly cluttered his cerebral cortex. He looked up at her beautiful smiling face; she was the angel that he'd been waiting for his entire existence.

"Me too."

Still, the images of The Cuck's features remained in the back of his mind, but Mickey was able to push them aside as he began to stroke his shaft while licking Ava's clit.

Suddenly, the madness that Ben had spouted off on the phone started to make sense. While he remained aroused and able to eat her pussy, a lingering feeling of dread slowly unfolded within him. It was exactly as he'd described. His mind understood and accepted that they'd come into the apartment alone, but he couldn't shake the feeling that he was being watched.

Mickey continued to try and focus; he couldn't blow his opportunity with a girl that he was so incredibly into. It was a miracle that they'd gotten that far in the first place. For a grunt like Mickey, the prospect was monumental. He used every ounce of his mental energy to move forward and insert his manhood inside the sexy girl he could only hope to have a future with. He kept his eyes on her, making a conscious decision not to let his gaze drift off into the uncertain darkness that surrounded them.

"Oh, fuck," Ava moaned, as her legs squirmed with pleasure.

Mickey continued to thrust himself in and out of her warm love. Her jubilation mirrored his own; she was every bit as into him as he was into her. He couldn't have been happier to see how much she was enjoying it.

Then it happened.

It started with a smell.

When Mickey's senses picked up the distinct odor, it was like an alarm going off in is head. The same smoky, repugnant scent that he and Ben had witnessed down in the basement. The same foul aroma that Ben claimed to have gotten a whiff of while he laid with Olivia earlier that day. It was potent and unmistakable. It was real.

"Oh, right there, that's so fucking good," Ava wailed.

Mickey continued pounding her with a machine-like, endless vigor. But as the smell overcame him, he couldn't help but turn his head in the direction it was coming from.

When his eyes came to the corner of his one-room flat, Mickey couldn't believe what he saw. The Cuck stood, lapping his glistening tongue in the air like an absolute loon. His belt buckle was undone, and his sore, over-stroked cock stared back at Mickey.

The Cuck's sharp and lengthy nails gleamed with wetness. The now claret-caked dead cells had accumulated a build-up underneath. It consisted of the scraped flesh he'd fished out from the gorge of gory horror that he'd hollowed out in his nightmarish, old manhood.

The juicy wads of his leaking member dripped, snugly tucked under his nightmarish fingernails that now looked stretched in almost hallucinogenic fashion. The old man continued rubbing his swollen member feverishly while his sable eyes drilled a hole into Mickey's soul.

A blood-curdling scream escaped Mickey as he fell over, on his side, and out of Ava. When he landed on the floor, the wicked image of The Cuck still remained in the corner, just a short distance away from him.

"Oh my God!" Ava cried, unsure what had happened.

"Wha—What the fuck?! How are you here?! What are you doing here?!" Mickey hollered, staring into the dark corner of his room.

"You invited me, what—what's wrong with you?"

The Cuck looked upon Mickey, continuing his motions as if nothing had happened, his spikey hand riding down his oozing shaft like a train on well-greased tracks.

"Get out of my house, you fuckin' cunt!" Mickey yelled, standing up and charging The Cuck.

He threw a swift haymaker at the old, disgusting face that glimmering saliva continued to rain down from. But just as Mickey's knuckles came up to his chin, The Cuck vanished. His fist smashed into the wall and a loud cracking noise could be heard pairing with the sheetrock snapping.

"Ah, fuck!" he cried.

Ava was already gathering her clothes when she interrupted his fit of madness.

"Okay, I'm cool with getting a little wild, but this is—it's too much. I'm—I'm gonna go."

Mickey laid on the floor holding his fractured hand, confused beyond all comprehension. The bucket of alcohol swishing through his bloodstream didn't help him rationalize what was going on. The room was spinning as fast as his heart was pumping.

Once he was able to realize what was happening, and that The Cuck had disappeared on him almost exactly as Ben had described, it was already too late. Mickey looked to Ava as she rushed to open the door.

"Wait! I'm, I'm sorry. I'm just really drunk," he explained, grimacing and holding his hand.

"I'm sorry, but I've gotta go, Mickey," Ava said, trembling while her eyes looked ready to water.

The shock that had been so suddenly introduced to her was too powerful to negotiate against; she couldn't escape the downtrodden flat fast enough. Ava slammed the door behind her, quite possibly slamming the door on their entire relationship.

AN AWFUL EPIPHANY

When Mickey entered Ben's flat, he was ready to apologize. What he'd initially believed to be exaggeration after a bender was somehow the stone-cold truth. The absurd picture he'd painted was replicated before his eyes, right down to the finer, most fucked-up details.

Ben looked like hell's husk. He sat wrapped in a blanket on his bed in a state of continuous shiver. His milky eyes were baggy and blackened around the edges from sleep deprivation. He presented the face of a man that was openly questioning his sanity. It was a face logged with a salty and weighty depression. Ben was so entrenched in his own agony he didn't even take notice of Mickey's heavily wrapped hand.

"You were right, mate," Mickey said solemnly. "You were right about everything."

Ben said nothing in response, he just stared forward at the wall, blank as a fresh sheet of paper.

"I'm sorry. I'm sorry I doubted you. I know it's real now. I believe you."

"It's getting worse," Ben said.

The apology seemed to fly over his head. It was the last thing he was thinking about.

"You've seen him again?"

"Olivia couldn't be bothered to come back here. It's understandable. You know me though, plenty of hens to pick from in my address book. But it's all the same result. And it's got me thinking… this is never gonna stop. It's never gonna fuckin' stop!"

"Just calm down, we'll—we'll figure this out—"

"What the fuck is there to figure out?! Do you realize what the fuck's happening?!" Ben cried out, as tears welled up in his eyes.

Mickey had never seen him so shaken. Ben was always a cocky prick; even the worst of situations that he'd been in always seemed like a breeze. Just the notion that he'd been so broken by this inexplicable series of events was beyond frightening. Mickey wanted to keep positive, but he couldn't help but feel like things were about to get a lot worse.

"Yelling about it ain't gonna change it none!" Mickey barked hypocritically.

"You know me, Mickey, I—I have issues. I need it. I need me ladies, can't live without 'em. I'll go mad. It's as simple as that. Feels like I've already gone mad. Like—Like I've relinquished a piece of my soul."

Mickey hung his head momentarily before returning his gaze to Ben's quaking frame.

"Just tell me what happened; I need to know just as much as you do now."

"Roxy came over, and at first, just like before, everything was fine. But right when we started in on each other, like fuckin' magic, he was here again! Except this time, I wasn't just seeing him anymore. I was seeing meself."

"What do you mean?"

"I kept getting these—these pictures in my brain of me. But I wasn't acting like me. I was acting a lot different."

"And what were you doing in these pictures."

"I was hurtin' meself. I was hurtin' meself *real* bad. I don't know how, but I know it was because of him. I didn't want to, but he—he forced me to do it."

"Jesus. At least it was just thoughts, aye? I'm glad you're alright. We'll figure it out, mate. We'll figure this out."

"I wish it was just thoughts," Ben replied, allowing the blanket he was wrapped inside to slide off his body and fall at his sides.

The reveal was ghastly; a sizable patch of the tender flesh on the top of his penis was blistered and somewhat charred. It still oozed a translucent fluid and remained in the early stages of scabbing. The horrific hotdog casing had been mauled, leaving it misshapen and disfigured. It was like someone had held a hot lighter flame on his privates for five minutes straight.

"Fuck almighty! What the hell happened?!" Mickey cried.

Ben was doing his best to hold it together and not completely unravel.

"He handed me a lighter and asked if I'd put the flame to me knob. So, I did."

More tears leaked out of his eyelids, as Ben drooped his head, disgusted with himself.

"Why the fuck would you do that?!"

"I don't know! I told you, he's gained influence over me! Either that, or I've just gone mad then, haven't I?"

"You haven't gone mad; I saw what you saw. So, unless we've both gone mad in a matter of forty-eight fuckin' hours we still have some hope."

"What hope could we possibly have?! I've just barbecued me fuckin' joystick, mate! So, you tell me, what hope could we possibly have?!"

Mickey thought about it for a moment, racking his brain, before deciding to open his mouth again.

"The only hope we have lies in the place that started all this shit."

Ben simmered his hysterics down and looked at Mickey.

"Bessie's?"

"We know exactly where this fucker is. There's a bit of urgency behind us figuring this out, fast."

"I—I don't know if I wanna go back. I don't even know if I can—"

"You can and you will! This piece of shit took Ava from me! He took my one shot! And I don't know how I'm gonna do it, but I'll be Goddamned if I don't give him one back."

Ben stared forward like he was being asked what he wanted for his last meal. Still unconvinced by Mickey's passionate words, he waited.

"Think about who you are, mate! You're the last one I expected to roll over so easy," he continued.

The last words that came out of Mickey's mouth finally seemed to register. They seemed to fall on the ears of the old Ben. The one that didn't take shit from anyone. The one who was the life of the party. The one who always projected a persona that was fearless.

"Alright, I'll do it."

Mickey looked satisfied with the breakthrough moment. But he might've been more grateful for Ben than himself.

"Good, because I wasn't asking. Whatever the fuck is going on, we're in this together now. You got me tangled in this fuckin' mess, you ain't leaving me to clean it alone this time. We'll go back tonight, the same way we did last time. Only this go round, that fuckin' cuck ain't gonna know what hit him."

Ben wiped the water from his eyeballs and molded his trembling lips into what was almost a smile.

In Mickey's mind, that was about the best he could've hoped for.

KNEE DEEP IN THE DREAD

The key remained in the same place as before. The same flowerpot holding a dead plant stared back at Mickey after slipping through the darkness behind the house. He tilted the stained pottery sideways and retrieved the worn key once again.

They had stormed back to the grounds just the way they had nights prior, their roles now reversed. This time, Mickey headed up the excursion with all the desire, urgency, and confidence to move forward. Ben trailed behind, unsure and anxious about the entire situation. Continuing to feel a bit sore from his ordeal, Ben stepped gingerly toward the bulkhead as Mickey tugged it open.

Darkness still saturated the cellar; it looked even glummer than their initial excursion. Mickey extracted a lighter from his pocket and flicked the spark wheel. The action caused Ben to recall the sadomasochistic act he'd recently performed on himself. A cruel grimace took hold of him, and he let out a quiet groan.

He could feel the burn of the flame.

He could see the skin on his pecker beginning to blister.

He could smell the singe of burnt pubic hair and the distinct aroma of roasting flesh.

"Sorry," Mickey whispered, looking back at his friend for a second.

They both peered into the darkness searching for The Cuck. It seemed inevitable that he'd be waiting, if not for them then for someone else. In their heads, they could see the creepy old fucker's face take shape in the obscurity. His wicked black eyes hung in the cold darkness. His chattering spiked enamel rattled relentlessly. His excited expression was overjoyed to see them. But it never came to be. If you stared into the darkness long enough, you could find anything, as was the case for Mickey and Ben.

Mickey continued to use the lighter to illuminate various areas of the old cellar. He seemed to become more agitated with each empty inch he revealed.

"Fuck, he's not here," Mickey whispered.

Ben was more relieved by the notion than enraged. He'd seen what The Cuck was capable of firsthand, and even though a badass like Mickey was by his side, for the first time in their storied history, he still felt nervous.

The Cuck wasn't just another loudmouth at the bar that needed some sense beaten into him. He wasn't some bloke with enough liquid courage inside him to start some beef. Ben didn't know what the fuck he was, and that was by far the scariest part of confronting him.

"Well, we tried," Ben replied, hoping that might be the end of it.

"He's probably upstairs," Mickey said, stepping closer to the staircase, ready to ascend.

"What are you doing?" Ben whispered.

"He ain't down here, so, the way I see it, there's only one other option."

"You—You think we should go back up there?"

Mickey gazed back toward his shaken friend; his face was one that meant business. He hadn't come to give it his best shot and walk away. He'd come to figure out what the next move was and didn't plan on leaving without being enlightened. If things had to get uncomfortable for that to happen, then, so be it.

He was scared, just the same as Ben, but that fear had been infected, and in turn, swallowed up by his rage. Mickey didn't have a little black book with an endless list of names that would spread their legs at the drop of a hat for him. He didn't have the luxury to be able to pick up a causal relationship with zero effort. His campaigns toward romance were taxing, strategic, stressful, and more often than not, heartbreaking.

"I don't think we have a choice anymore," Mickey coldly replied.

As a unit, the duo formed an odd mixture of anger and fright, but despite their contrast in emotions, they both climbed each step with extreme caution. They could certainly agree that neither of them was aiming to create a stir. The element of surprise could be their best asset in such an unpredictable circumstance.

Once they reached the top of the steps, Mickey scanned the area but saw no one. Darkness clouded the quarters, seeming as thick as smoke, and the entire first floor was quiet as a funeral.

The door to Bessie's room was cracked open slightly, calling to them. Just like the hallways, blackness shrouded the bedroom, same as it had upon their first trip. As Mickey's heart thrashed inside his chest, he whipped out a switchblade from his coat pocket and proceeded forward.

"What the fuck is that for?" Ben whispered.

"Just in case," Mickey replied, ejecting the fat chrome blade from its home.

He readied his knife in one hand as he gradually widened the opening with the other. When the gap was large enough to enter, they stepped inside.

Bessie laid in almost the exact same position as she did when they'd left her before. She remained blindfolded and a slave to her sweat stained mattress. She was in the nude again (maybe she always was), her lumpy extremities and flab visible to whoever decided to walk inside her room.

"Teddy, is that you?" Bessie purred.

"Guess again," Mickey replied, a cold-hearted tinge now clinging to his dialect.

"Mickey! I couldn't forget that voice. But you—you sound a tad different—"

"Cut the fuckin' shit, Bessie. Tell me where he is?"

"Where who is?"

"Listen to me and listen carefully. I don't have time for games. The old man, your husband, where is he?"

"Who?"

"The Cuck, whatever the fuck you wanna call him. Tell me where he is, or you'll not like what comes next."

Ben watched on, still dealing with his own trauma; he was a ball of nerves. Just like every other time shit went sideways, Mickey took the lead. His assertiveness offered him a taste of comfort, a feeling that had seemed so distant over the past couple of days.

"Mickey, I—I'm not married, I don't know what you're talking about."

"Don't fuckin' jerk me around, Bessie, I'm begging you. Don't make me do something I'm gonna regret."

"It's the truth. Look at me. Do you see a ring on my finger?" she asked, holding her large hand up.

Mickey examined it and also the nightstand beside her. A heavy confusion quickly clouded his mind.

"Then who takes care of you?" he asked, trying to poke a hole in her story.

"There is a live-in nurse, a woman named Candace that lives upstairs. Why do you think I asked you to keep it down when you came last time around?"

Mickey pondered the question but remained silent.

"She doesn't know what I've been up to, about the key outside or the ad. This phone," she explained, pointing to the one by her bedside, "is a separate line from the primary. I just leave it off the hook until I feel like seeing someone. She's none the wiser. Thank God because I don't think Candace would feel comfortable staying here with so many strange men in and out of the grounds. But I just need to feel something. *Anything,* really."

The darker emotions that Bessie had been holding in silently for so long bubbled up to her face. She'd silenced them for so long, she avoided thinking about reality. They remained above her head like pesky gnats that she snuffed out almost daily with the strange sex. It filled the void both figuratively and literally. It helped her forget the living hell that was her life.

"I'm dead inside. There's nothing going on. I'm just here. I know it's selfish. I know I'm wrong. But I don't care. I'm tired of being a prisoner in my own fucking body."

Ben and Mickey glanced at each other in disbelief. The bizarre story of monumental depression was all too relatable. While physically they each varied drastically, mentally, there was much common ground to be shared.

"I know it's dangerous. I know any one of you could come in here and slash me to ribbons. But maybe that's part of it. Maybe that's part of me. The part of me that wouldn't mind it. The part of me that would welcome it. Because this isn't life. This isn't sane."

Ben couldn't control the shaking of his body. The woman's warped words were so miserable that they could only be authentic. Bessie's broken tone, undeniably horrific situation, and sense of defeat were all genuine. There wasn't a single positive factor within her boundaries that made disputing it with her worth perusing.

"I think she's telling the truth," Ben whispered, leaning into Mickey's ear.

"We'll see," Mickey replied, nodding his head.

Ben took a step back from Mickey and brought his back closer to the wall beside the doorway. An unsettling feeling continued to bubble inside him, raging even harder than before. The woman's story was so dark. It was something that Ben never aspired to be associated with, yet, somehow, there he was. The realization that one shit choice had drawn him into such a sinister black hole was overwhelming.

"That's why I wear the blindfold," Bessie continued. "I just don't wanna see it coming. You can understand that, can't you? Just because I'm okay with death doesn't mean I'm not afraid of it. You know, when you came inside, you sounded so much angrier than the other night. I was sad at first, but then kind of excited. I thought you might be the one. What did you imagine doing to me? Maybe you were thinking about strangling me? You know, you still can, if you want to."

"What the fuck?"

The voice that came from the doorway behind Mickey and Ben wasn't familiar. The man was middle-aged and creepy, like the spawn of an uncrowned serial killer. The criminality of his appearance seemed impressed upon his chromosomes. His general nature suggested he was a man of the darkness. His greasy hair and ugliness startled Mickey as he turned around with the blade still firmly in hand.

"Teddy, I was wondering when you'd arrive!" Bessie excitedly exclaimed.

"I knew this was a fuckin' rip off!" Teddy said, glaring at the shiny steel blade in Mickey's palm.

Teddy reached into the pocket of his stained trench coat and extracted a revolver. The compact, chrome piece with a wooden handle elevated swiftly up to Teddy's eye level. He stared down the top of the barrel, his dirty thumb cocking back the hammer assertively. It was second nature to him.

Before Ben or Mickey could make heads or tails of what was transpiring, the shot had already rung out. A single bullet, intended for Mickey, flew over his shoulder, missing him by inches.

Instead of the intended target, Bessie's skull absorbed the slug. The hot steel pushed through the front of her face and an eruption of thoughtful tissue splattered the dingy wall and oak headboard behind her. She laid motionless, her wish from just moments prior coming to a fatal fruition.

"Crazy bastard!" Ben yelled, lunging for Teddy's firearm as he attempted to ready a second shot.

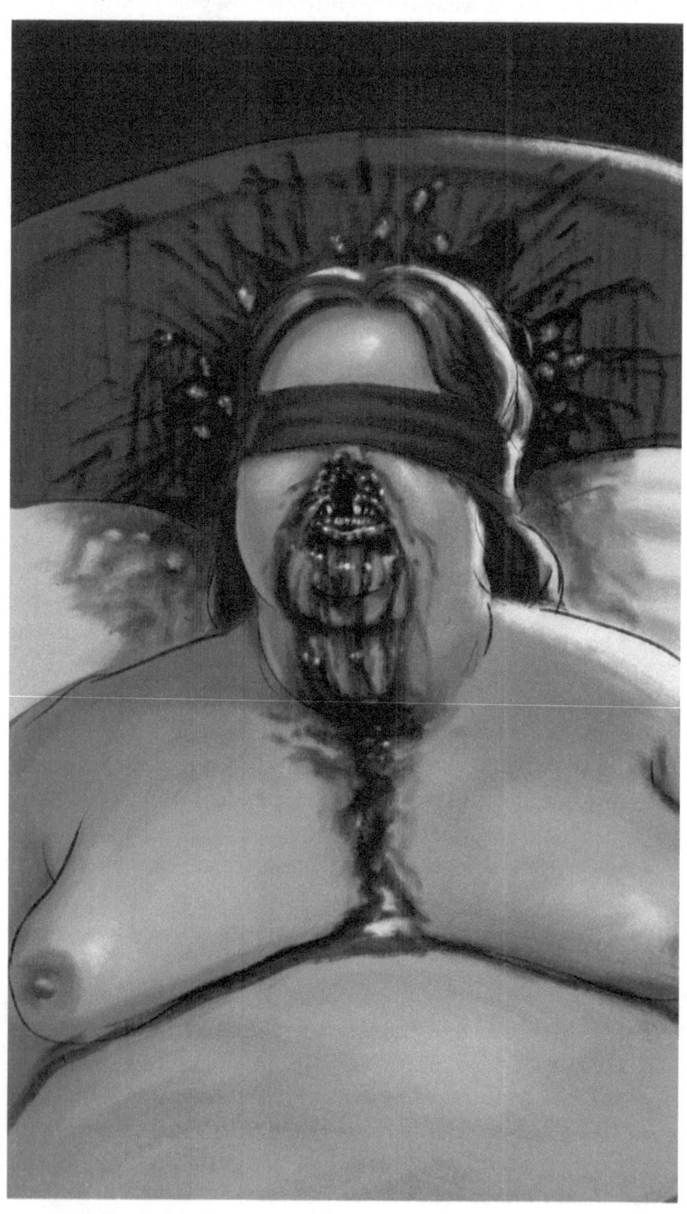

The two struggled while Mickey gathered his bearings. He charged forward, attempting to avoid stepping in front of the smoking barrel of the revolver as best he could. The five-inch knife he clenched readily disappeared into Teddy's abdomen, creating an excruciating distraction that allowed Ben to wrestle the gun away from the thug's killer grasp.

Teddy cried out as Mickey mined the knife out of his entrails, and quickly reinserted it, deeper than the first stab. He jostled the unforgiving metal within his guts, creating a substantially larger opening than the initial hole.

Mickey gritted his teeth and continued to scramble Teddy's innards as he watched blood begin to find its way out of Teddy's lips. Lost in the moment, the wound opened to gaping dimensions, as a hearty stream of red evacuated the criminal's frame and crimson saliva dribbled down his chin.

"Mickey! Let's get the fuck out of here!" Ben cried.

"Bessie?! What was that? Is everything alright down there?" a female voice that they could only assume to be the live-in nurse's came from above them.

They both scrambled to their feet, trying not to slip in the puddling blood in cartoonish fashion.

Mickey reluctantly removed the knife from Teddy's gut one last time, but as he considered running, he found himself compelled into another act. This act would be a final act, as Mickey applied a gracious amount of pressure and ran the stained blade across Teddy's neck. The newly carved out carnal orifice expelled a flood of essence that there would be no coming back from. Or so Mickey hoped…

"What the fuck?!" Ben cried, shocked by his sickening barbarity.

He knew Mickey wasn't the one to fuck with, but the man's cold-blooded execution wasn't something he could've fathomed seeing at the start of the evening.

They bolted down the cellar steps and through the bowels of the house. They were both so panicked by the violent onslaught that Mickey didn't even ignite the lighter for guidance. Instead, he felt around, making his way to the bulkhead door from which they'd entered.

When they busted out of the basement, Ben's prior injuries suddenly seemed to vanish. The adrenaline shot and unparalleled fear gave him a dose that kicked his body into a gear he hadn't been aware he harbored.

When they entered the night again, Ben slipped the bloody gun into the pocket of his jacket and shifted his gawk of horror back to Mickey.

"What the fuck do we do now?!" he pleaded, begging for Mickey to provide some direction.

Mickey collapsed the ruby red switchblade and looked at him, every bit as frightened by the horrific turn of events.

"We run!"

MASTURBATORY MENACE

"Why'd you fuckin' kill him?" Ben asked, putting the last of his bloody garments into the garbage bag.

Mickey finished sliding on one of Ben's spare shirts and looked up at him. His face was anything but happy. There was a coldness in his eyes that seemed to be resurfacing with regularity as of late.

"We didn't have a whole lot of options."

"I had his bloody gun! You—"

"And what would we have done had the nurse come downstairs? He saw our fucking faces, Ben! Think! He blew Bessie's goddamn brains all over the wallpaper! I didn't exactly have a choice!"

"He killed Bessie, not us! We were just protecting ourselves."

"Would you prefer to be explaining that to the bobbies right now, or be standing here free? Because I imagine they might not think we're a pair of upstanding citizens heading back from plowing a morbidly obese woman in the middle of the night. I imagine they'd be trying to find whatever fuckin' slant they needed to stick that on us."

"It isn't right."

"I'm not saying it is."

"Then why'd you do it?! What you don't realize is that when you killed that bloke, it wasn't just you committing murder, it was the both of us! We'll both go down for it!"

"Have you ever seen a gun before, Ben?"

"What does that have to do with anything?!"

Ben was still really worked up, but Mickey was at a boil. He just had more control over his emotions than his friend, but his patience was wearing thin.

"Because you live in a country that no longer allows them. What kind of people do you think carry guns now?"

Mickey was calm, but it was almost to a point that was frightening. Ben was beginning to see that.

"I imagine—"

"It was a rhetorical question! They're the underbelly of society! The killers, you fucking twit! What do you think would've happened if that fella would've survived? You think he would've thought we were square? Or do you think you'd have spent the rest of your life looking over your shoulder? Maybe you're okay living like that, but not me!" Mickey screamed, not allowing him to finish his answer.

"Splendid, so instead we'll spend the rest of our lives looking out for the cops instead? We could've just told them the truth—"

"The truth means nothing! It's what you can prove, mate. You think that the world is this fair place, where everything balances out, but you've been sheltered! You've never been nicked, you don't know how it works because you've had blokes like me around, always bailing your soft ass out! Well, I'm tired of fightin' your battles. I'm not riskin' my hide just so you can fuckin' sleep at night. I'd rather be looking out for a pair of handcuffs than a fuckin' knife in me back! You're wearing me thin, Ben. The ice is about to crack, and you ain't gonna like what's underneath it. You gonna listen to me on this, or are we gonna have a scrap?"

Ben remained silent. He was still shaken from the extreme and unexpected violence. It seemed that it was becoming a trend.

"Good, keeping that mouth shut is about the smartest thing you could've done tonight. Now tomorrow, you're gonna go to work like you normally would. You're gonna be the same bloke you've been every day of your life; a charming little smart-ass. Then you're gonna come back here and hide this gun in the boot of your wagon, drive out to Humber Bridge, and set it free. Understood?"

Ben nodded his head somberly, like a child that had just been taken to task by a relative.

"I'll take care of the bloody clothes and me knife. Then tomorrow, this'll all be in the rearview and we can move on. We can forget about it all like some bad dream."

Mickey gathered up the garbage bag and tied it off. He bowed away from Ben and headed back for the door.

"Mickey."

He turned back to Ben, annoyance still lingering on his face.

"What?"

"What about The Cuck?"

"We'll deal with him next."

***

When Ava removed her top, her breasts looked voluptuous. Mickey used his good hand to squeeze around the nipple, then pinch gently at the edges of her areola. Her bare ass smacked down against his hairy thighs, as she rode him with additional force to drive his prick further inside her.

"You feel so good, you feel perfect," she moaned.

She placed her hands on his chest and leaned forward, rubbing her tits in his face. Mickey happily accepted the offering; opening his mouth and using his teeth to nibble on the end of her breast. His eager tongue circled her flesh repeatedly like cars on a racetrack.

Ava pulled away, continuing to ride him while hanging her head forward. The angle made it so that her black hair obscured her entire expression.

But Mickey longed to see her face; he was teetering on climax and desired to lock eyes. They had to lock eyes.

He gently pushed up against Ava's breasts with both loving hands, causing her to lean further backwards. Moonlight trickled in through the cracked window, offering an impossible sight.

The face that was fixed upon the petite pair of shoulders in front of him was no longer that of Ava; it was a heaping glob of distorted gore, the last image that Bessie had left upon her abrupt and brutal farewell. The jiggling hunks of facial tissue and fractured mandible made their way down her tits, some of the human gunk even dropping onto Mickey's face and into his mouth.

She emitted a blood-curdling shriek that shredded his eardrum with ease. It was hard to believe the noise was even coming out of such a mass of mutilation. Her ruined facial features looked closer to a scrap pile on the floor of a slaughterhouse than any human he'd ever seen.

The moans of madness and pain were so profound that they jolted Mickey's body and caused him to tense up. When his eyes opened, Mickey was grateful he'd been ripped callously from the dreary dreamscape, but the brain ache hadn't concluded.

Mickey found himself pressing one hand against his thrashing heart and the other on the snooze button of the screaming alarm clock by his bedside. His erection looked up at him, as stiff as the rigor mortis that Bessie was undoubtedly dealing with at that very moment.

It pleaded with him like a dog that wanted a treat. It acted independent of his brain, begging without shame or reserve. His body tended to separate the frequent miscues of his life from the pleasure he sought to derive. If he didn't tuck it away in a box and forget about it, he'd never have a moment of enjoyment.

It's a shame to waste a good erection. No matter how shitty things get, life keeps going. It can always get better. But a hard-on is only around for so long… Mickey thought.

While the thought of the morbidly obese woman's dissolving face surely wasn't the cause of Mickey's cock-sure morning wood, the perverse parts where Ava made an appearance most certainly were. It was the most incredible dream until the nightmarish reveal. He stepped closer to the mind frame that it would be tragic to waste such a gift.

Mickey hadn't been with a woman as drop-dead sexy as Ava at any point in his existence. He was so close, but now, the probability had plummeted through the floor.

Going to have you one way or another, Mickey thought, unable to resist the idea of her a moment longer.

He pulled down his wrinkly boxers and wrapped his fingers around his hard cock. As he closed his eyes, he tried to return to the images from the dream. He ran his fingers up and down his solidified shaft, stroking with a thoughtful touch that only he could apply with such perfection.

This updated, nightmare-free version of Ava looked perfect in his mind. Every inch of her was just to his liking. Her figure was so delicious and curvy that pre-cum was leaking out of him almost immediately. Instead of his rough and cracked hands upon his manhood, he envisioned her perfectly manicured nails wrapped around him.

The vision was everything he wished, until, suddenly, it wasn't. A different image, one that he hadn't been thinking about, slipped into his mind in place of the fantasy. The devilish shift now controlled his direction without request. The swift domination of his mind left a pathetic, submissive feeling that he'd never been accustomed to dwelling in his sickened psyche.

Mickey was alone now and naked. He stared into the long mirror that was a few feet in front of him. In his left hand, he held a set of poultry shears, while using his right to elevate his penis away from his testicles. He positioned the scissors at the top of his scrotum and readied the metal to meet. Slowly, he started to pull his fingers together. He watched on in horror as the space that separated the shears from his skin became less and less.

Just before the skin opened up, Mickey's eyelids peeled apart. The reality was every bit as disturbing as the vision that had been funneled into his head. There he stood, in front of the mirror, nude, with poultry shears resting mere millimeters from detaching his balls from his body. The birth of the incision felt inevitable, but somehow, he was able to hold back.

Even more alarming than the ghastly act of self-harm that Mickey was on the verge of committing, was the revolting, old chap cackling in the corner. The evil elder was the reason he was in this mess. He'd returned.

"Cut 'em, lad! You won't need them anymore! They're my bullocks now!" The Cuck yelled.

Due to the morning sky radiating through the window, there was more lighting in the apartment. The environment allowed his otherworldly features to become more visible than they'd ever been before. There were demonic elements to The Cuck's appearance that would be soul-shaking for anyone unfortunate enough to cast their gaze upon him.

The lost eyes of oblivion.

The spikey, decaying dentures.

The pointed red nails.

The maimed bloody cock.

The Cuck's smoky smell once again found Mickey's nasal cavity. The stroking of his sharp fingernails around his gore-drenched zipper was hypnotic. Some kind of sick mindfuck of a trick.

Mickey remained motionless, the sharpened shears still nestled around his nuts, the razor edge now firmly enough against him that it was slicing into his sack.

He couldn't pull his eyes away from the revolting rhythm of the fiendish cuck; the process was like pulling two powerful magnets apart.

The carnal lubrication galore.

The furious nails scratching like a dog gone mad.

The sinister strokes of an ill mind.

The slippery, blood-soaked shaft of his spotted pecker.

Mickey tried his damnedest to fight the unnatural urge that he'd been impregnated with. It took using every ounce of energy within his body, mind, and soul to finally be able to draw his manipulated focus away from The Cuck's disgusting body and rabid fingernails.

When Mickey's head jerked away, he let go of the shears and fell to the rug. His frame was sore from holding the same pose for many minutes. There was nothing left to fuel even the most basic action. He lingered on his knees, exhausted in a way that was unrelatable to any moment in his past.

He was spent, but even more than that, emotionally overwhelmed. Just like anyone might be after finding a way to cheat death.

A VISCERAL VISIT

Mickey had been calling him for the last two hours, but no matter how many times he punched in the digits, Ben's voice didn't manifest. It took him some time to feel semi-normal again after The Cuck's most recent appearance.

He was now able to recall that both he and Ben had some serious fucking problems on their hands. Problems in the real world as well as the frightening one they'd just been introduced to. These issues were life-altering. They weren't petty things that would be put to bed one way or another; their complexities were a tier that stretched beyond the bounds of the worst things Mickey had ever found himself wrapped up in.

Initially, he hadn't understood the severity of what Ben had been through. Mickey hadn't felt the power of The Cuck's insidious inspiration, nor the hapless feeling that lingered within one's mind after being shown the darkness. He considered that if he had another encounter with the demon, his nuts might very well be on the rug next time, or worse...

I didn't even know I was doing it. I was just there. How can it be possible? How can it be real? Mickey questioned, as he stared at the telephone, wondering if he should pick it up again.

He'd never thought about mutilating his body until that morning. The absurd excitement and eagerness he'd experienced when those shears were up against his scrotum weren't his own.

It was manufactured.

"He should've been home from work hours ago. I don't like it," Mickey said aloud, restlessly pacing around.

He looked at the keys on the table and then back to the phone at his bedside. The decision was obvious; he needed to go and see Ben. He needed to make sure that the gun got dumped. Also, more importantly, Mickey knew that Ben's life was at risk from an angle that he might not even be aware of.

Despite still being a bit sore at him over the prior evening's disagreements, Ben was still his best friend.

If that little pervert rips one off, he'll be done for...

"One more," he whispered, first picking up the keys, before moving back over to the phone.

When the buzzing on the line began, Mickey expected the same thing as before; no answer. What he got was far more shocking—the unmistakable, sadistically seasoned voice of The Cuck invading his ears.

"Come on over, lad. Your friend needs you. He needs you soon. I need you…"

"You son-of-a-bitch!" Mickey cursed.

He turned to the coatrack and slipped on his jacket. Feeling around in the front pocket, he located the switchblade he'd cleaned off the prior evening. Mickey quickly extracted it from his coat and made sure the blade still ejected properly.

"Good thing I haven't gotten rid of you yet," he said to himself.

A thought popped into Mickey's head and left his face slated with a sour expression.

"The fuck is this gonna do to him anyhow?"

The question was relevant. He decided to take it anyway. Even if he couldn't use it, he would still need to be rid of it.

Mickey thought about The Cuck's disgusting tone from just moments prior, but he didn't allow any time for the chill that ran down his spine to set in. Instead, he slammed the phone into the receiver and raced to the door.

***

When Mickey arrived at Ben's house, he readied the spare key that he'd been given some time ago. But when his hand took hold of the doorknob, he realized he wouldn't need to use it; the door was closed but unlocked.

With caution contorting his approach, Mickey slipped inside, and shut the door quietly behind him. Ben's house looked normal enough, offering a privacy that was alien to Mickey since he'd been regulated to single room apartments for the majority of his life.

Mickey carefully inspected the premises, and oddly, nothing seemed out of place or amiss in any of the rooms he ventured into.

There were no signs of a struggle, but then would there be? The bad things that infected Mickey's mind with worry weren't things that would come from others, they came from within.

"Ben?" Mickey called out, vigilantly weaving his way in and out of the various rooms.

The kitchen was empty.

The parlor was empty.

The office was empty.

The bedrooms were empty.

"Ben? Where are you, mate?"

As he continued to creep through the well-organized areas, the concern in Mickey's inflection only grew. Eventually, he realized that the bathroom was his last remaining option.

The ajar amber door gave off an ominous vibe. Mickey's heart was pushing blood through his body almost as fast as it had during the prior night's atrocities.

When Mickey's fingers gripped hold of the knob, he held his breath. The instinctual illness in his stomach screamed in advance. As he reluctantly pushed open the barrier, he was confronted with a portrait of pure horror.

Ben laid back in the tub, white as a sheet, and every bit as motionless. His eyes were left frozen in a gruesome gawk of terror; like he'd seen a ghost. Probably because he had.

A large, ruby-glazed kitchen knife lay on the bathmat beneath Ben's limp fingers. It was undoubtedly the instrument that was responsible for tainting the half-filled bathwater.

The river of crimson that had evacuated Ben's lifeless corpse dominated the fluid. It wasn't initially evident where the blood had come from, until Mickey's eyes landed on the piece of Ben that was still floating within the sinister soup. The top part of his cock looked as he remembered it upon Ben's reveal—partially burned and blistered.

"BEN!" Mickey cried, rushing over toward the vomit-worthy blood-tub.

Mickey shook him by the shoulders as the panic set in. He adjusted his fingers to search for a pulse, but it was long gone. The familiar cold and clammy skin that had so often sat beside him for a pint after work would never do so again. They would never share another laugh or enjoy each other's company. Ben was now elsewhere.

Mickey's body began to feel the tears and fear that would be generated when most entered a room with a dead loved one. It hit hard.

"Fuck, fuck, shit!" Mickey cried.

"I like the first two…" The Cuck's voice said, suddenly manifesting in the room.

Mickey didn't look behind him, he just froze.

"Forget him, just forget him," he whispered to himself, trying to focus.

Mickey would've liked to have taken a moment to grieve and try to ward off the hurt; but his situation was far more complicated.

Can't call the law; there's no way to sanely explain this. They'll come to me eventually... Maybe? They might ask what I did last night. Got to get me story straight. THE GUN! Got to get the gun!

Mickey had no other choice but to leave his friend dead and alone. There wasn't much he could do to help him in his state of decay anymore.

It didn't take Mickey long to locate the gun. Ben had cleaned the blood off it and slipped it into a plastic bag inside his dresser. As Mickey lifted up the back of his coat and tucked the gun into his waistband, he caught a reflection in the mirror affixed to Ben's bureau.

The Cuck's thin tongue flickered in his mouth and his black eyes locked on Mickey.

"You're next, lad!" he barked with a cackle.

The next-level fright that overcame Mickey assisted in fueling his flight. He turned away from the dresser and headed in the other direction towards the front door. On his way out of Ben's house, The Cuck's smoky aura did it's best to coax him back inside. But he avoided focusing on him and was able to break free. As he hauled ass down the street, and back to his car, he counted his blessings that no one was outside.

***

Mickey stood at the mid-point of the Humber Bridge. The sky had gone gloomy, much like his day. His heart still ached for Ben. Never had he felt so utterly alone. Not only was Ben his only outlet, but he didn't deserve such an end. No one did.

As he looked over the edge, Mickey tried to decide if he should throw the gun or himself over the rail. Running from demons (metaphorically and literally) was no way to live. He was no fortune teller, but when he pondered his future, the projections all seemed to spell the same thing. He was set for a life of chaos and calamity. A fear-drenched existence that was too insane to explain.

He'd never had a picturesque life, but he found a way to get on and be content. A way to cherish the little things he was given. A pint here, a good laugh there. So much of it seemed improbable now.

Mickey removed the gun from his pocket and opened the plastic bag. He looked at each end of the bridge before turning the plastic upside down. He watched on with a frown that held back emotion as the gun fell, plunging into the massive body of water below.

OUTREACH

Mickey sat in his chair in front of the television. The show that was playing on screen depicted a man and woman clearly smitten with each other. Once they began to kiss passionately and embrace, Mickey reached for the remote and flipped the channel. Anything associated with carnal desire remained a dark door that he wasn't willing to open.

Initially, he'd thought that there was no 'help' or salvation for a man in a predicament such as his. The only safeguard he'd figured out before it was too late, was to permanently distance himself from anything sexual. So, that's exactly what he did.

Over the course of the next few weeks, The Cuck's voice would find him from time to time. He might randomly slip into bed and get a whiff of his smoky scent or catch a faint glimpse of his horrific features beside his reflection. But with Mickey remaining bored and forlorn, The Cuck seemed unable to influence him as he'd done previously.

It wasn't as if Mickey had been able to bag any girl on the block, but he did enjoy masturbating quite regularly. He'd been forced to put the kibosh on that. It sucked but it worked. It was better than waking up one morning and cutting his own nads off in front of the mirror.

At times, he wondered if jerking off was Ben's undoing. There was no way to know for sure. He might have been done with sex at the moment, but he wasn't done trying to figure out what the fuck was going on.

As Mickey turned off the television, the phone rang. Mickey pulled himself up from the couch to answer it.

"Hello?" he answered with reluctance; there weren't any calls that he was expecting for the foreseeable future.

"Mickey?"

"Who is this?"

"It's Ava."

"Oh, Ava… didn't expect to—to hear from you."

"You never explained what happened that night…"

"It's not important. I'm sorry I lost me head. Sorry you had to see that. But what's done is done, I suppose."

"Why don't you come around for a coffee anymore? I miss seeing you."

"I've just been really busy, but you're right. Maybe I can do that sometime. Maybe."

In his mind, he knew he was offering up a pipedream.

"I know things didn't go as planned last time, but maybe we can try again. Just get dinner this time, no drinks?" she asked, with a giggle.

Her candor was surprising. She seemed so forgiving, like she really saw something inside of him. She was sweeter than syrup.

Mickey paused for a moment. His expression screamed that there was nothing he wanted more than to take her up on the offer. But the agony on his face explained that he knew he couldn't.

"I'm not sure that's a good idea. I'm—I'm in a bit of a pinch right now, Ava."

"Oh… well, maybe some other time then?"

"Maybe. But in the meantime, keep an eye out for me at The Bean Shop, okay?"

"Okay, Mickey."

"Cheers, darling."

"Cheers."

The phone went dead, and Mickey dropped it back down on the receiver as his heart simultaneously dropped to the pit of his stomach. His disdain for what he'd just done couldn't be hidden. The one woman he'd wanted most actually liked fucking him. It would've been so much easier if she didn't. But nothing had come easy for Mickey, and that didn't appear to be something set to change.

He looked down at the handwritten note that was on the nightstand beside the telephone. The scribble had an address at the bottom of the sheet and at the top it read: 'ASM Saturday at 1 PM.'

***

"I—I don't know why I want to do it—or not do it, I guess, is the way I should say it. All I know is I'm all done," Chris said, proudly looking at Mickey, and the rest of the group.

"It's okay, you don't have to explain why. If that's the way you feel, then that's all we need to know. And we support you. One-hundred-percent we support you, mate," Thomas delicately replied.

"Well, now that I'm done with sex, I guess I can shoot for the Nobel Prize," Chris said with a laugh.

"Cheers," a man replied.

The rest of the room let out a chuckle that blended in with their soft applause. Those in the group all seemed quite comfortable with each other. There was no need for pretentious peacocking, and no ulterior motives, just the flat-out truth. In a strange way, Mickey enjoyed the first gathering far more than he ever imagined.

"Alright, excellent meeting. Feel free to chat a bit before we close up shop, and I'll see you in a couple weeks," Thomas said, finishing his slow clap.

Mickey followed suit, fading out his mild applause while keeping his eyes fixed on the group leader.

There were no informational resources that Mickey was

able to find regarding anything like the events that he and Ben had experienced. He had no choice but to speculate and venture outside the box. The only clues he was granted were within his own behavior.

In examining his personal patterns, Mickey found that he'd essentially become asexual. The only thing he imagined might shed light on his absurd situation was the people following the same pattern as he was.

The group was nearly two hours away, but there was nothing left to do anymore but chase answers; no matter how offbeat they might seem.

As the rest of the folks in the meeting dispersed and chatted, Thomas took notice that Mickey hadn't taken his eyes off him.

Another member of the group approached him and began to strike up a conversation, but Thomas quickly wrapped it up.

Still not breaking his glare with Mickey, Thomas approached and said, "Follow me."

They stepped out of the main gathering space and into a side office with a single green desk lamp lighting it. Thomas closed the door behind them and smiled at Mickey.

"So, how was your first go round?" Thomas asked.

"It was good. Nice to see folks getting the demons off their shoulders."

"Hmm," Thomas said, stroking his chin.

"What?"

"That's an interesting way to put it."

"What do you mean?"

"Your choice of words are telling."

"I'm sorry, I didn't mean to be crass—"

"No, you weren't. It's not that it's—do you mind if I ask why you're here?"

"I'm here because I'm—I'm done. Just like the other bloke said. Not really sure why."

Thomas grinned and shook his head.

"Am I missing something?" Mickey asked.

"I don't think you're being truthful with me. It's okay if you're not. I understand. You're scared."

"Why would you say that?" Mickey asked, confused by his response.

"I've been doing this for some time now, and in my vast experience, the majority of people that join this group are naturally nonsexual. Something that their born with or an ideology that they come to love. But then there are others. A smaller minority. But they ain't coming of their own free will. They ain't coming because they want to. They're coming because they have to. I hate to say it, but you strike me as the latter, mate."

Mickey's eye sockets stretched so far it looked like they were giving birth.

"You've seen it. You've seen the demon. I know you have because I have too," Thomas whispered.

"Yes," Mickey said, holding back tears. He'd felt so alone the last few weeks. The isolation seemed like it would never end with Ben out of the picture. All that remained were questions about sanity and relentless fear. Suddenly, those dreadful feelings had been lifted, at least momentarily.

"What—What is it?" Mickey begged for the answer through a shaking jaw.

"It's exactly what you think it is. It's a cuck. Best we can figure it, these cucks are some kind of parasite. All of the encounters that I've been privy to seem to have a lot of eerie similarities."

"How do you mean?"

"Did it ask you for permission?"

"Permission?"

"Permission to watch you?"

Mickey nodded his head, shamefully.

"I figured. First, they ask for permission to watch, and then leech onto you during the actual intercourse. From most of the stories that I've heard, they're usually contracted during sexual acts of a more extreme and bizarre nature."

"What do they want?"

"It's hard to say. But nothing good, I would surmise. When you have sex or toy with yourself, they manifest in full strength. The faintest whiff of promiscuity draws them in, sure as stink on shit. That burning desire for a partner is always correlated to that smoky scent. That's when they're dangerous. Eventually, the more the cuck appears in that state, the more it implants dark ideas, genital mutilation being the most common. They seem to take great pleasure in that regard. The more you open that door to indulgence, the more danger awaits you. Those who fall off the wagon or choose to continue on with a sex life haven't historically lasted long. So, it's good you've found us."

"What happens to them?"

"They're brainwashed into oblivion. They become putty in the cuck's malformed hands. They're manipulated into unspeakable acts. You know already; you wouldn't be here if you didn't."

A horrific image of Ben and his mutilated cock floating in the tub flashed in Mickey's skull. *You left him to rot in the bathtub,* he thought.

"So, ultimately, it becomes a simple choice. You can live without the slightest semblance of physical love… or die chasing it."

"There—There's no way around it?" Mickey asked, feeling more emotions stirring inside.

"I'm afraid not, mate," Thomas somberly replied. "It's not as if this is a topic that can be publicly acknowledged. It's too fuckin' bonkers for anyone to believe it. You only believe it when you see it for yourself."

His eyes widened with past trauma.

"The longer you abstain, the longer you'll go without seeing it. The Cuck will still be out there, looking for others, but it'll never forget about you completely. I've had mine for over twenty-six years now. But, like anything, you learn to live with it."

Like anything? Mickey thought, blown away as ever. *Jesus Christ…*

Thomas could see the heartbreak in Mickey's eyes, the syphoning of his soul from his physical form.

"Don't be too down, it gets better. Eventually, it just becomes background noise. We know exactly what to do to avoid their influence, but that doesn't necessarily make it any easier."

Mickey wasn't sure what to say to him. He didn't expect to understand the exact workings of the mess he'd found himself ensnared in after a single visit. The enlightenment was heartbreaking.

Thomas could see the doubt and dread in his expression. He remembered the same weight falling upon his own shoulders when he was a bit younger. Thomas extended his arm and placed his palm on Mickey's shoulder.

"It's gonna be alright, mate. You'll see. It just takes some time."

BACK TO THE BACKPAGES

The Cuck walked awkwardly down the slick street, his odd body bobbing side to side like some kind of foreign entity had just been injected into his skin.

The downpour of rainwater matted his thinning hair and dripped around the sides of his face. His sharp teeth still leapt out of his jaws, but not in a way that was so obvious that he was something otherworldly. He squinted through his glasses that were heavily dotted with rain before slowing his pace near a telephone pole.

He was breathing heavily and adjusted his long, black trench coat before squatting down. The Cuck pulled open the door of the metal receptacle beside the phone pole and snatched up one of the numerous free papers that were housed inside it.

Without hesitation, he quickly flipped through the bulk of the primitive periodical to the back-pages. As he glared down at the print, he tried to use his soaked coat to shield the water from completely destroying the inky pages.

His long, yellowed fingernail slowly made its way down the column, and en route, it passed one offering that read: 'CALL FOR FREE FUN. LOOKING FOR A MAN WHO DOESN'T MIND LARGER LADIES.'

Bled that one dry, The Cuck thought, quickly moving past it. He was aware that the ad, while still in circulation, was no longer a viable candidate for him.

The Cuck wasn't bothered by the revelation; he knew that there were plenty more ads to pick from. And he took comfort in knowing that every month or so, there would be a brand-new batch pressed.

His pointy spear of dead cells slid a few inches down, stopping over a patch of wording that read: 'HUNGRY LAD WANTED. MUST BE OPEN-MINDED. MUST BE WILLING TO GRADE & DEGRADE OTHERS.'

The Cuck grinned, his freakish teeth expelling a surge of saliva that was excessive, even for him. His brain began to race; the idea tickled him something fierce.

Now that sounds like a nice bit of fun, he thought.

ABOUT THE AUTHOR

Aron Beauregard is the three-time Splatterpunk Award nominated author of such abominations as "The Slob," and "Beyond Reform." This is the first story he's specifically written for the screen, but certainly not the last. He'll continue to expand his brand of dark storytelling to the live-action realm. So, if you're a filmmaker and you've found yourself intrigued by this work, or any of his others, please send serious film inquiries to:
AronBeauregardHorror@gmail.com

**THE CUCK 2: HUNGRY LAD
CUMMING SOON?**